Max's Words

by KATE Banks

pictures BY Boris KULIKOV

FRANCES FOSTER BOOKS ✂ Farrar, Straus and Giroux ✂ New York

Distributed in Canada by Douglas & McIntyre Ltd.
Color separations by Chroma Graphics PTE Ltd.
Printed and bound in the United States of America by Phoenix Color Corporation
Designed by Robbin Gourley and Vera Soki
First edition, 2006
16 15 14 13 12 11

www.fsgkidsbooks.com

Library of Congress Cataloging-in-Publication Data
Banks, Kate, 1960–
      Max's words / Kate Banks ; pictures by Boris Kulikov.— 1st ed.
          p.   cm.
      Summary: When Max cuts out words from magazines and newspapers,
collecting them the way his brothers collect stamps and coins, they all learn about
words, sentences, and storytelling.
      ISBN-13: 978-0-374-39949-8
      ISBN-10: 0-374-39949-2
      [1. Language and languages—Fiction.   2. Collectors and collecting—Fiction.
3. Storytelling—Fiction.]   I. Kulikov, Boris, 1966–   ill.   II. Title.

PZ7.B22594Max 2006
[E]—dc22
                                                            2005045070

To my Max

– K. B.

No ! To my Max

– B. K.

Max's brother Benjamin collected stamps.
He had stamps of many colors and sizes.
They had ragged edges and sticky backs.
Some had famous people on them.
Others had places or buildings, or flowers or trees.
Benjamin spread his stamp collection across his desk.
He showed it to his friends and family.
Everyone admired it.
Max said, "Can I have a stamp?"
"No," said Benjamin.

Max's other brother, Karl, collected coins.
He had coins of many sizes and values.
They came from different countries.
Some were silver-colored with rough edges.
Others were copper-colored with smooth edges.
They were all shiny.
They had people and buildings on them
and the year in which they were made.
When Karl showed them around,
everyone admired them, too.
Max said, "Can I have a coin?"
"No," said Karl.

Max wanted to collect something, but he wasn't sure what.

He gave it some thought.

Finally he said, "I'm going to collect words."

"Words?" said Benjamin. He laughed.

"Very funny, Max," said Karl.

Max began collecting small words.

a, *The*, its, *an*, a*te*, **WHO**, *to*, and, **BUT**, was, in, *On*, **OUT**, big, see, ᵞᴼᵁ, **DAY**

He cut them out of magazines and newspapers.
And he spread them across his desk.

Pretty soon Max found bigger words.
HUNGRY, ASKED, THROUGH, ALLIGATOR, CROCODILE, hissed
He cut them out and added them to the others.
Max's collection grew rapidly.

Max collected words that made him feel good.

PARK, BASEBALL, **DOGS**, Hugs

He collected words of things he liked to eat.
BANANAS, **PANCAKES**, *ice cream*
He collected words that were spoken to him.
Good morning, *goodbye*, go away!

He collected his favorite colors.

green, BLUE, Brown

Max opened the dictionary and found words he did not know.

He copied these on small slips of paper.

slithered

IGUANA

"What are you doing, Max?" asked Benjamin.

"Let me see," said Karl.

Max's collection grew too big for his desk.

So he spread out his words on the floor.

He separated them into neat piles.

When Benjamin and Karl arranged their collections
in different orders, it didn't make much difference.
But when Max put his words in different orders,
it made a big difference.

A BLUE CROCODILE ATE The green iguana.
THE BLUE iguana ATE a GREEN CROCODILE.

Soon Max's collection of words spread into the hallway.

Sometimes Max gave away a word or two.
SEE YOU later, **ALLIGATOR.**
HAVE a NICE *DAY*.

When Benjamin put his stamps together, he had just a bunch of stamps.
When Karl put his coins together, he had just a pile of money.
But when Max put his words together, he had a thought.

MAYBE i COULD TRADE a word For A stamp OR A coin.
Please?

"No," said Benjamin.

"No," said Karl.

"I've got one thousand stamps," said Benjamin.

"When I get a few more coins, I'll have nearly five hundred," said Karl.

"And when I have a few more words, I'll have a story," said Max.

"A story takes a lot of words," said Benjamin.

"I know," said Max.

"You don't have enough," said Karl.

"Let's see," said Max.

Max sorted through his words. He picked out a few and began arranging them on the floor.

ONCE & There WAS little BROWN worm WHO wished TO BE A BIG green SNAKE.

A BIG green SNAKE.

Benjamin and Karl stopped what they were doing and came over to look.

Max continued his story.

THE worm

slithered Through

the

GRASS. it stuck out

ITS tongue and hissed

LOUDLY.

LOUDLY .

Max stopped to choose some more words.
Benjamin butted in.

Then
ALONG CAME
a BIG mean
GREEN
CROCODILE

Then it was Karl's turn.

"I'M HUNGRY,"
it said .

Benjamin grinned. He chose a few more words.

THE crocodile OPENED its mouth WIDE and

Karl scrambled for more words.
He wanted the crocodile to eat the worm.
But Max was quicker.

The LITTLE brown WORM DARTED down A hole, GLAD To Be a WORM.

"Hey, I want another story," said Benjamin.

"So do I," said Karl.

"And I want a stamp and a coin," Max reminded them.

"Oh, all right," said Benjamin. He gave Max a stamp.

Karl gave Max a coin.

And Max gave them each some words.

And kept the rest for himself.

once There WAS a BIG BROWN

the END